Rapunzel and the Drop of Doom

by Nadia Higgins   illustrated by Meredith Johnson

magic wagon

visit us at www.abdopublishing.com

Published by Magic Wagon, a division of the ABDO Group, 8000 West 78th Street, Edina, Minnesota 55439. Copyright © 2009 by Abdo Consulting Group, Inc. International copyrights reserved in all countries. All rights reserved. No part of this book may be reproduced in any form without written permission from the publisher.

Calico Chapter Books™ is a trademark and logo of Magic Wagon.

Printed in the United States.

Text by Nadia Higgins
Illustrations by Meredith Johnson
Edited by Patricia Stockland
Interior layout and design by Rebecca Daum
Cover design by Rebecca Daum

Library of Congress Cataloging-in-Publication Data
Higgins, Nadia.
  Rapunzel and the Drop of Doom / by Nadia Higgins ;
illustrated by Meredith Johnson.
      p. cm. — (Fiona & Frieda's fairy-tale adventures)
  ISBN 978-1-60270-575-3
  [1. Fairy tales—Fiction. 2. Characters in literature—Fiction.]
I. Johnson, Meredith, ill. II. Title.
  PZ7.H5349558Rap 2009
  [Fic]—dc22

                                    2008038265

For Yvette, my kind of princess—N. H.

Fiona

Frieda

Chapter 1

Once upon a time in a land not far away at all (in fact, just a short ride from the Sprinkledust County Fairgrounds), there lived two third graders, Fiona and Frieda. Some grown-ups got the girls mixed up. They'd call Fiona Frieda and Frieda Fiona, and you really couldn't blame them. The two best friends were almost always together. Plus, there was the fact that both girls were well known for their active imaginations. For more than sprinkles, more than fake tattoos, more than waterslides, and even more than staying up late, Fiona and Frieda loved fairy tales.

But grown-ups who knew the girls well—and most kids—could easily tell them apart. First of all, Fiona was the one with glasses. But there were other obvious differences, too.

Fiona and Frieda were always playing a game they'd invented called Fairy-tale Adventures.

That meant they were usually pretending to be characters from fairy tales. So if you said something like, "Cute shoes!" to Fiona, she'd probably curtsy really low and reply, "You're too kind." That's because she was being something like a princess or a fairy or a noble village girl.

But if you said "Cute shoes!" to Frieda, she might say, "Poof!" and pretend to turn you into bacteria. Then (because she wasn't mean in real life), she'd pause the game and explain that the wicked witch, beast, or whoever she was being, didn't like the word *cute*.

Today was the first day of summer vacation, so Fiona and Frieda weren't technically third graders anymore. But when they were third graders, something amazing had happened to them. While they were playing Fairy-tale Adventures, they discovered that they had magic rhyming powers.

For example, if Fiona said "la-la-la" at the exact same time Frieda said "cha-cha-cha," magic sparkles would surround them. All the everyday noises of their lives would stop. Now only their voices and those of real fairy-tale characters could be heard.

That's right. Though Fiona and Frieda's world looked the same on the outside, it had in fact become a magic realm of fairy tales. The girls would be inside a real fairy-tale story—and they knew what was going to happen.

Of course, they couldn't just sit back and let the witch poison the princess or put everybody under an evil spell. So it was always up to Fiona and Frieda to save the day. Sometimes things got so scary they wanted to use their magic rhyming powers to go back to normal life. So far, though, they hadn't ever missed a happy ending.

Today wasn't just the first day of summer vacation. It was also opening day of the

Sprinkledust County Fair. And this year, the girls got to do something they'd never been allowed to do before. This year, they wouldn't be stuck at a quilting exhibit or listening to a talk about window screens with one of their parents.

No, the girls would finally have their chance to split up from the grown-ups.

Once inside the county fair, Fiona's mom handed Fiona a cell phone.

"Call me if you run into *any* problems you can't handle," her mom said.

"Certainly," Fiona said, using her most responsible voice.

"And you girls stick together," her mom added.

"Yes, Mother." Fiona nodded several times.

For a while, her mom looked at the girls with squinty eyes. Finally, she walked away and stopped turning around to look at them.

For a minute, the girls just stood there. They let the crowd part and stream around them. They took all of it in—the roller coaster zooming overhead, the pink clouds of cotton candy, the crash of drums coming from a nearby stage.

"Smell," Fiona whispered. She loved "fair smell," a mixture of grass, french fries, and farm animals.

"Mmmmmm," both girls said together.

Fiona and Frieda were free to do anything they wanted. What would they do first?

Fiona knew. She was already at the end of the block, joining the long line snaking around the french-fry stand. What better way to enjoy the fair than with the delicious, yummy, tempting treat of fair food?

Fiona waved to her friend. Then Frieda found her own place at the back of a long line at the ice-cream booth. She made a mean witch face at Fiona, who pretended to shoot her with a bow and arrow. That pretend game made the line go by so fast that, before she realized it, Fiona was up at the beginning of the line.

"Small curly fries, please," Fiona said. In a second, she had a paper cone filled with hot, golden-brown fries. She popped one into her mouth. "Oh, I forgot!" She turned back toward the girl behind the counter.

At that same moment, it was Frieda's turn at the ice-cream counter. "May I please have a—," Frieda began.

Exactly as Frieda finished her sentence with "chocolate malt," Fiona made her request for "extra salt."

Later, the girls would figure out that it had been the rhyme of chocolate malt/extra salt that had accidentally triggered their magic rhyming powers. Soon they'd be really glad for the accident. But at this very moment, Fiona and Frieda grumbled as the magic sparkles filled the air.

"Chocolate malt! Extra salt!" Each girl shouted at the high-school kids behind the counter. But they knew it was no use. The girls were in the magic realm of fairy tales. They could only be heard by fairy-tale characters now.

Chapter 2

Fiona and Frieda ran toward each other, pushing their way through the silent crowd. But even before they met up, each girl stopped short.

Craaaaaaack!

A sharp sound split the air.

The girls looked at each other. The noise wasn't coming from either of them.

Craaaaaack!

What was that? The sound itself meant that a real fairy tale was taking place, right there at the county fair. But which one was it?

Craaaaack! Fiona and Frieda followed the sound past the bumper boats, a noiseless talent show, and a field of tractors.

As the noise got louder, the girls' surroundings looked less and less familiar.

"Where are we?" Fiona wondered aloud. She felt the phone in her pocket and, for a second, thought of the promise she'd made to her mother. She smiled, though, when she remembered: *Here, in the magic realm of fairy tales, all rules of normal life don't count. Besides,* she thought with a giggle, *my mother wouldn't be able to hear me anyway!*

"Check it out!" Frieda said. She pointed to a fun house with giant, leafy trees standing on either side of a dark tunnel. Above the tunnel was a sign with letters that looked like gnarled branches. It read, Forest of Fear.

"I can't believe we've never seen this before," Fiona said. After all, the girls knew every other part of the fair like the clothes in each other's closets.

"This ride is Stop Number One right after we solve this mystery," Frieda said.

But before Fiona could say, "You're on!" the girls came upon more new stuff: an owl fact board, a grizzly bear display, a camping-supply exhibit. Then, around the corner from a moss experiment, they came upon a vast garden.

"What's this?" Frieda wondered. It was too big to be some sort of gardening contest.

"Maybe it's where they grow food for the fair workers," Fiona guessed.

Frieda examined the plants. She recognized sweet peas and mint as well as pumpkin vines and a blueberry bush. But most of the garden was given over to a kind of dark green lettuce. Rows and rows of green dots continued beyond the top of a hill.

Frieda picked a leaf and sniffed. She took a nibble. "Spicy!" she said.

Meanwhile, Fiona continued up the hill.

"Frieda! Frieda! Come quick!" she called out. She was pointing at something in the distance.

Frieda scrambled toward her friend. "What is it?" she shouted.

There, at the end of the long rows of vegetables, was a tall structure pointing into the sky.

The sound continued to get louder as the girls approached the structure. The sound changed, too. Now it went *Craaaack! . . . Thud. . . . Craaaack! . . . Thud.*

Craaaaaack!

A white object made a graceful arc from the tower to the fields below.

Thud.

The girls ran toward it.

Fiona picked it up. "It's a baseball, Frieda. Somebody's batting balls from the top of the— what is that thing?" she asked.

As the girls got closer, Frieda said, "I think it's some kind of ride." She squinted at the sign at the bottom and read, "Drop of Doom."

"It's one of those free-fall rides!" Fiona squeaked. She'd been waiting years to be old enough to go on one. "See that cage? It's like an elevator that carries you to the top. Then the whole thing drops super fast. Look! The cage is at the top now. It's going to drop any second!"

The girls watched, but the cage didn't move. It stayed up there, like a ball stuck in a tree.

Craaaaack!

Another baseball shot far off into the garden. But now, in addition to the crack and the thud, Fiona and Frieda heard a voice going, "Yesssss!"

"That sounded like a girl!" Fiona said.

"Fiona," Frieda hissed, "somebody's up there!"

She was suddenly glad she hadn't had that chocolate malt. It felt like somebody was squeezing her stomach from inside.

"Come closer." Fiona grabbed Frieda's hand. If Fiona was scared, she didn't show it. But her muscles felt all jumpy like a bag of rubber balls.

What they saw next, though, made even Fiona shiver a little. For there was no teenager to run the ride at all. On top of that, the controls were all rusted and strung with cobwebs.

"Frieda," Fiona said, "that cage doesn't move. That girl's been stuck at the top . . . *maybe for years!*"

There was no question now. The girls had stumbled upon a real fairy-tale emergency— and they were pretty sure they knew which one it was.

"A girl in a tall towering thingy . . . ," Frieda began.

"Past all kinds of forest stuff . . . ," Fiona continued.

"Next to fields and fields of spicy lettuce, which must be . . . ," Frieda said.

"Rapunzel!" both girls said together.

Chapter 3

In the Rapunzel story from the library, a humble woman and her husband live next door to a mean witch. The witch happens to be some kind of amazing gardener. Her haunted castle is surrounded by gardens, which, in turn, are surrounded by a high wall. It's pretty clear that this witch prizes her veggies more than anything else—especially other people's feelings.

Well, the humble woman gets pregnant and, just like on TV, she starts craving all kinds of weird food. It just so happens that from her upstairs window, this poor woman has a fine view of the witch's beautiful garden. So—you guessed it—she starts craving the witch's veggies. In particular, she pines away for just a taste of rapunzel—some kind of fairy-tale lettuce that witches and pregnant village women must like.

"Oh, husband," the wife says, "if you don't bring me some rapunzel, I shall surely die!"

So the husband has no choice. It's not as if the witch is going to send him some rapunzel in a gift basket. He has to sneak into her garden and steal it.

Of course, she catches him.

He explains to her about how his wife is going to die without rapunzel. The witch makes a deal with him that, at first, seems really nice. She says he can pick as much rapunzel as he likes as long as he gives her something in return.

People in fairy tales must not read very many fairy tales, because next he says something that you should really never say to a mean witch. He cries, "I'll give you anything!"

Then, after his wife gives birth to a beautiful baby girl, the witch shows up and reminds the husband of his promise. Her evil plan reveals itself in all of its brilliance.

The husband realizes that you can never go back on a promise to a witch. Over his wife's wails and screams, he hands over their baby to the witch.

The witch names the baby Rapunzel. The books usually say that the witch raises Rapunzel "as her own." Apparently, that's not saying very much, because, for one thing, the witch never lets Rapunzel get a haircut. So her hair grows so long that it drags on the ground behind her. Plus, she never lets Rapunzel have any friends. Then, when Rapunzel turns 13, the witch locks her away in a tall tower. The tower has a room up high with a window. It has no door and no stairs, so Rapunzel can never leave.

In the books, it never says how Rapunzel got up there in the first place. But that fairy-tale mystery was now perfectly clear to Fiona and Frieda. "The witch sent her up in the cage and then turned off the ride!" Frieda said.

It was satisfying to have that mystery solved. But, there was still much to come. Had the prince shown up yet?

Fiona and Frieda couldn't stand the thought of Rapunzel stranded on top of the Drop of Doom. More than anything, they wanted to rescue Rapunzel right away.

But they needed more information. How would they get Rapunzel down? How would they outsmart the witch? Where, for that matter, was the witch?

"Well, we'll find out soon enough," Fiona said.

Anybody who's ever read *Rapunzel* knows that the witch shows up at the tower every day at the same time. She has a special way of getting up to visit her prisoner. She stands at the base of the tower and calls—

"Rrrrrraaaaaapunzel! Rrrrrraaaaaapunzel!" A high, crackly voice rang out from the other side of the garden.

"The witch!" Frieda hissed.

"Get down!" Fiona whispered, pulling her friend down with her. They scanned the garden for a place to hide.

"Asparagus!" Frieda pointed to a small patch of her favorite vegetable. Soon they were peering out through tall green stalks at one of the most famous fairy-tale scenes of all time.

Frieda's heart was pounding like a dance video. But now her fear was being pushed out by something even stronger—curiosity. As a fan of witches, Frieda was especially excited by this witch. The books didn't say much about her.

Frieda had always wondered: Why did the witch want a baby in the first place—especially if she was going to be so mean to her?

Every artist drew the witch differently, and Frieda herself had drawn her many times and in many different ways. But Frieda had to admit that in real life, the witch looked nothing like she'd expected.

With a frizzy mop of hair sticking out of a big straw hat, the witch looked like, well, an ordinary grown-up. Besides, her clothes were all wrong. She had on tan shorts, a blue tank top, and—were those purple clogs? Frieda couldn't help feeling a little disappointed.

For her part, Fiona couldn't wait to catch a glimpse of Rapunzel. Of all the fairy-tale heroines, Rapunzel probably had it the worst. What did she do all day in that tower, anyway? She must be so lonely and sad.

"Rapunzel! Rapunzel!"

The witch's shouts interrupted the girls' thoughts. The wicked woman was standing at the foot of the Drop of Doom.

"Let down your hair," she shouted, "that I may climb it like a stair!"

At that, a long, long, black braid tumbled down the Drop of Doom. *Wait a second. What about fair hair?* Fiona wondered.

"Hummmmph," the witch sighed. She pulled out a pair of leather gloves from her back pocket and slowly put them on. Then, she grabbed the braid with both hands and with big, wheezy breaths, she climbed. One arm, *pffffffff,* another arm, *pffffffffff.*

Fiona giggled. She looked at her friend. How come Frieda wasn't laughing?

Then Fiona realized what was wrong. "It's okay," Fiona said, patting her friend's shoulder. The witch's face was as red as clown lips now. "She's still probably a really great witch."

The witch's legs were flopping all around like broken Slinkies. She was trying to get a foothold against the tower, but when she finally got her feet against the metal, her clogs fell off. "Raaaapunzel!" the witch shouted. "Help!"

Rapunzel's hands appeared by the window, and she started pulling up the braid. At last, the witch made it to the top, and the braid was whisked back up.

There was nothing the girls could do now but wait for the witch to go—and to think. But Frieda didn't want to think the thoughts that were in her head. *What if Fiona was wrong? What if this witch turns out to be a dumb, boring witch? What if—?*

She especially didn't want to think the thought that was the most worrisome of all. *What if I don't like this fairy tale after all?*

Chapter 4

At last Fiona and Frieda saw the sight they'd been waiting for—the witch climbing down the braid. She stood again at the foot of the tower, straightening her hat. *Whoosh.* In a second, the braid was on its way back up.

Fiona and Frieda watched until the witch was out of sight. Then they crept up to the tower. Usually during a fairy-tale emergency, the girls had to think hard about a plan. But this time their next move seemed so obvious they didn't even have to say it out loud.

"Go ahead. Say it," Frieda told Fiona.

In the story, the prince hears Rapunzel's wonderful singing and follows her voice to the tower. Then, just like them, he sees the witch climb the braid. Once the witch is gone, all he has to do to get up the tower is do what the witch did.

He says, "Rapunzel, Rapunzel, let down your hair." Rapunzel does, and he climbs up.

It seemed so easy in the story. But now that it was their turn, the girls weren't sure what to do.

"She won't recognize my voice," Fiona said. The girls thought about that for a second. "Will she still drop her braid for me?" Fiona wondered.

"Well, in the story, she drops it for the prince," Frieda said, "which means . . ."

"Rapunzel let down her hair for a *stranger!*" Fiona said.

"You're right!" Frieda said. The girls had never thought of that before. "And then, when Rapunzel first sees the prince, she trembles with fear!"

"That's not okay!" both girls said together.

There was something else that bothered Fiona. "And don't you think it hurts to have her hair climbed on like that?"

"Maybe," Frieda said.

The girls agreed that they would definitely have to find out before climbing up the tower.

First they walked way out into the garden, so that Rapunzel could see them easily from her window. Then, to make sure that the princess would be able to hear them from that far away, they shouted together.

"Rapunzel! Hi! Yooo-hoooo. Rapunzel! Over here!" While the girls shouted, they jumped up and down and waved their arms.

Rapunzel's figure soon appeared behind the window. "May I help you?" the damsel slowly asked.

"I'm Fiona!" Fiona shouted.

"I'm Frieda!" Frieda shouted.

"We want to rescue you from the tower!" the girls shouted together.

At that, Rapunzel gasped a little and covered her mouth with both hands.

"How do you know me?" Rapunzel called from the window.

"We're fairy-tale experts!" Frieda shouted.

"We saw the witch!" Fiona added.

Rapunzel was quiet for a second. She was too far away for the girls to see her expression, but they guessed she was observing them and wondering what to do.

"We need to talk. Can you climb my braid?" Rapunzel said at last.

"But doesn't it hurt?" Fiona asked, walking closer to the tower.

"It used to," Rapunzel admitted. "But now I have a trick so it doesn't. I'll show you when you come up."

"Then we'd love to," Frieda said, smiling.

At that, Rapunzel jumped a little and said, "Woooo-hooo! This is so exciting! I've never had guests before."

Fiona and Frieda looked at each other. Another mystery solved: That meant the prince *hadn't* come yet.

Soon the black braid was dangling in front of the girls.

"I'll pull from my end," Rapunzel yelled. "It helps to climb the side of the tower with your feet."

Frieda took hold first. She pulled with her arms and pushed with her feet as hard as she could. Then Fiona grabbed on and did the same. It was a good thing both girls liked practicing on the climbing wall at gym. With all their muscle power, getting to the top was as easy as tic-tac-toe.

Chapter 5

At the window, Fiona and Frieda saw how Rapunzel had her braid tied tight around a hook.

"So that's how it doesn't hurt!" Fiona said.

"I see," Frieda said, pulling hard on the iron hook. "The hook bears the weight instead of your head."

"It was actually Violet's idea," Rapunzel said, untying her braid from the hook.

"Violet?" Frieda asked.

"The witch," Rapunzel explained.

"Violet?" Fiona mouthed at Frieda, trying to cover her smile with a pretend cough.

But Frieda couldn't laugh. She didn't think that was a good name for a witch at all.

Rapunzel was done untying her hair and turned toward them. "Come on in," she said.

At last the girls got a good look at the real live damsel, and now it was Fiona's turn to be confused. Rapunzel didn't look like the books said at all! First of all, her long, long braid wasn't blonde. And, it snaked out the back of a baseball hat—and not even a pink or purple one. Plus, she was wearing just a plain T-shirt and green shorts. And was that a chocolate stain? Fiona looked down, trying not to stare. That's when she noticed that Rapunzel had on one light blue and one dark blue sock.

Rapunzel saw Fiona notice, because she pointed at her socks and giggled. "I couldn't find any matches in my sock drawer."

At that, Fiona had to smile. "That always happens to me, too!" she said. "That's why I'm wearing sandals today." She pointed to her own silver sandals with butterfly straps.

"Cute shoes!" Rapunzel said.

Frieda expected Fiona to curtsy and say something princess-y, like "Why, thank you ever so much!" But for some reason Fiona wasn't using her princess voice. Instead, she just grinned and said, "Thanks!"

"Make yourselves at home," Rapunzel said. She pointed to some chairs against the wall.

Now the girls were even more surprised, for Rapunzel's room didn't look at all like the prison cell they imagined it to be. It was, well, *comfortable*. There was soft furniture (beanbag chairs!), pictures on the wall, and, through the only door in the tower, a bathroom.

"I'm having an orange soda. Would you girls care for one as well?" Rapunzel offered.

"Yes, please," Fiona and Frieda said.

As Rapunzel dug inside a cooler, the girls walked over to the window. There was a ball stand, bats, and an orange crate filled with baseballs. One of the balls was made of yellow foam.

Rapunzel handed the girls their drinks. She saw the foam ball in Fiona's hand. "That's the one I used for practice when I was little," she explained, "when I first became a baseball fan."

"But how—?" Frieda began to ask.

But Frieda didn't know how to say it without making Rapunzel feel bad.

"You mean, how do you become a baseball fan when you're stuck on top of the Drop of Doom without any friends or a phone or a TV?" Rapunzel asked Frieda's question for her.

Frieda's face turned a little pink. "Ummm, well, yeah."

"Come here." Rapunzel pulled the girls over to the window. "Stand right here and look way over to the right." The girls peered in the direction of Rapunzel's finger.

Fiona saw it first. "The Sprinkledust Sprites baseball stadium!" she said.

"You know it, lady!" Rapunzel said, holding out her hand to Fiona for a high five. "I can see all the games from here."

Rapunzel smiled dreamily as she looked out at the stadium.

"Someday I'm going to join a real baseball team," she said. "That's why I've got to keep up on my batting practice." With her chin, she pointed to the crate of baseballs.

Fiona looked at all the balls dotting the witch's garden. "But how do you get your baseballs back?" she wondered.

"Violet brings them to me," Rapunzel said. "She brings me all my baseball stuff."

"No, no, no." Frieda shook her head at Rapunzel. "She's a mean witch! She can't do nice things!"

"Why not?" Rapunzel asked, tilting her head a little.

Wow. Here was a fairy-tale question that Frieda had never, ever thought about before. She had no idea what to say, and she didn't like that feeling one bit. Even more, the question filled her head with all kinds of other questions she didn't like.

Frieda couldn't help but wonder, *If a mean witch did enough nice things, could she become nice? Could fairy-tale characters really just switch like that?*

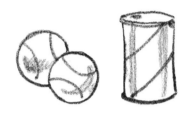

Chapter 6

"Soooo," **Frieda** said, still reeling from Rapunzel's question. "If Violet's nice, then why doesn't she let you go?"

Rapunzel leaned forward and crossed her arms.

"It's really weird, Frieda," she said. "It's almost like Violet can't figure out whether to be nice or mean."

She looked out the window for a second. "I've asked her why she won't let me go, but she never answers me. She just pretends she doesn't hear me or changes the subject or gets mad instead. I keep hoping that one day she'll let the cage drop, but I can't wait any longer." Rapunzel pulled out a doodle-covered notebook from under one of the beanbag chairs. "Ready to brainstorm?" she asked.

In all caps she wrote F & F & R'S ESCAPE IDEAS across the top of a page. Then she piled her braid into a ball and cozied up in her own hair.

"I have some ideas. Number One," Rapunzel read aloud as she wrote, "make hang glider. But what could I use?"

"Your hair?" Fiona said the first thing that came to mind. "Weave it into giant wings off the sides of your head . . ."

"I love it!" Rapunzel giggled. "But it sounds dangerous."

"Not if you had feathers and hollow bones," Frieda said, which gave her another idea. "Number Two: Trick Violet into turning you into a bird!"

Rapunzel laughed even harder. "Or an insect!" she added.

Fiona was twirling her hair around her fingertip. She was thinking about the fairy tale and how the witch tricked Rapunzel's father.

"Violet's too smart for that," she said.

"You're probably right," Rapunzel agreed. "Plus," she added, "I really like being human."

"Me too," Fiona said, giggling. "Especially the being smart part."

Then Frieda thought of something else. "You know," she said, "I doubt Violet's magic is even powerful enough to turn you into an animal. I mean—think about it. She has to climb your braid to get up here."

"Good point," Rapunzel agreed. "I bet the wicked fairy from *Sleeping Beauty* could just wiggle her nose or something and zip right up here in a cloud of smoke."

Now it was Fiona and Frieda's turn to laugh—and to be amazed. "You know about Sleeping Beauty?" Frieda asked.

"Of course!" Rapunzel said. "And I speak English, too, you ding-a-ling." She pretend punched Frieda on the shoulder. "Though I'm not sure *Sleeping Beauty* is my favorite fairy tale."

"What *is* your favorite fairy tale?" Fiona asked.

"Or favorite witch?" Frieda asked.

"And favorite princess?" Fiona added.

"Let me think! Let me think!" Rapunzel said, laughing.

And so began one of the best conversations Fiona and Frieda had ever had. As they talked, the doodle-covered notebook was soon forgotten.

"Have you read your *own* fairy tale?" Fiona asked at one point.

"Oh, no, that's the one fairy tale Violet won't ever, ever let me read," Rapunzel said. "Have you read it?"

Chapter 7

And so the girls began to tell Rapunzel her own story. They started with the lettuce and her pregnant mother who craved the leafy vegetable known as rapunzel.

"How horrible!" Rapunzel exclaimed when they got to the part about the witch tricking her father.

Rapunzel looked so troubled that Fiona quickly fast-forwarded the story to the prince part.

"And then the prince hears your beautiful singing from the tower," Fiona said.

"Singing!" Rapunzel laughed so hard she had to cover her mouth to keep from spraying orange soda on the girls. "I sound like a walrus with a toothache when I sing!"

That's when Fiona and Frieda had to explain how the books, though helpful in fairy-tale emergencies, weren't always exactly right about everything.

"So—let me guess," Rapunzel said. "The prince rescues me?"

"Well, not exactly," the girls had to admit.

"But he does bring you silk scarves every day so that you can make a ladder," Fiona said, "though you never get a chance to finish it."

"Because the witch finds out about him and cuts off your braid so he can never climb up to see you again. Then she kicks you out," Frieda added.

As if to protect it, Rapunzel grabbed the ball of hair beneath her. "Kicks me out?" she asked slowly.

All of a sudden it was like those cartoons where a lightbulb pops up in the air above someone's head. Only this time there were two lightbulbs. For as Rapunzel said those words, the perfect escape plan took shape in the minds of Fiona and Frieda.

"The hook is already there!" Frieda said.

"All we need are scissors!" Fiona added.

"You're right," Rapunzel said, twisting her braid around her wrist. "It would be the perfect plan to cut off my braid, tie it to the hook, and climb down, but . . ."

"But what?" Frieda tapped her foot impatiently.

"But what about Violet?" Rapunzel said.

"Don't worry about her. You never see her again once you leave the tower," Frieda said.

"Never see her again?!" Rapunzel exclaimed. Her mouth was getting all quivery. "So who lives with me?"

"Well, you're kind of by yourself for a while," Frieda said.

"Until the prince finds you," Fiona put in, cheerfully.

"How does he find me?" Rapunzel asked.

"He hears you singing," Fiona said.

"I'm doomed!" Rapunzel burst into tears.

Fiona sat down next to the damsel and hugged her a little, while Frieda went to get Kleenex. The girls had to admit—if they were Rapunzel, they'd be just as scared.

"Wait a minute," Rapunzel said at last. She sat up and wiped her nose with the back of her hand. "Why did you say the witch cuts off my braid, again?"

"Because she's jealous of the prince," Fiona said.

"She doesn't want you to have any friends," Frieda added.

A slow smile spread across Rapunzel's face. "But now I do have friends!"

Suddenly, she hopped to her feet, picked up a beanbag chair, and playfully whammed it at Frieda. The girls were so stunned, they didn't even defend themselves when Rapunzel sprayed them with a water gun.

"It's a sleepover party!" Rapunzel said. Then she started pouring popcorn into a pan. In between the *pop-pop-pops*, she explained, "Violet will be back first thing in the morning. She'll see you here with me and . . ."

Frieda finished Rapunzel's thought, saying "She'll be so mad. She'll cut off your braid in a fit of jealousy!"

"Exactly," Rapunzel said. "And when she does, you girls grab that braid and hold on tight until I say so. Then Violet will be stuck in the tower just like us. She'll be forced to help me. I'm not running away until Violet sets things right."

Chapter 8

"Rapunzel! Rapunzel!"

"Huh? . . . What?" The girls woke up at the sound of Violet's voice.

"Rapunzel! Rapunzel!"

They rubbed their eyes. The morning sky was just beginning to glow.

"Rapunzel?" The voice was starting to sound worried.

"It's her! She's here!" Frieda said.

Fiona jumped up and planted her feet by the window. She curled her hands into fists. "I'm ready," she said.

Rapunzel slowly gathered her braid, tied it around the hook, and let it fall. The girls heard Violet's heavy breathing and the sound of her shoes scraping against the metal. The sounds got louder and louder until—

"Rapunzel!" Violet yelled from just below the window. "I've been calling and calling. Where were you? Is everything okay?"

Rapunzel pulled Violet into the room. "I was asleep," she said. "You see, I was up late last night."

She spoke louder, "I was having a pajama party with my new friends, Fiona and Frieda."

Now Violet was standing in the room. She looked straight at Fiona and Frieda, and then she sighed and plopped down on the floor.

"Oh, fern fronds!" Violet said, putting her head in her hands. *Sniff.* She wiped her nose on her sleeve. Was that? Was she . . . *crying?* Fiona and Frieda inched closer.

Violet looked up at them and held out her hand. "I'm Violet," she said. "Please excuse my manners."

My manners? If Fiona and Frieda were reading this in a book, they'd be giggling and snorting. But here, in real life, they didn't feel at all like laughing at this rumpled witch.

"I knew this day would come," Violet said at last. "Of course, I always expected it would be the prince, but it doesn't matter. I still have to choose."

"Choose?" Rapunzel put her hand on Violet's shoulder.

Violet looked up at Rapunzel. "Yes, choose. Do I follow the fairy tale or not?"

"You mean—you know the story, too?" Rapunzel asked.

Violet sat up. "Oh, yes, I suppose Fiona and Frieda must have told you. It's a very famous one," she said. "A very good one, too, which is why I hate to just let it go. Especially after all these years of keeping it up, you know, for the sake of our readers."

"Keeping it up?" Rapunzel asked.

"Of course! Why do you think I've been keeping you up here in a tower all these years? You don't know how many times I've dreamed of taking you to a baseball game! Or taking you on a tour of my garden! Or just a ride on the Ferris wheel." She laughed a little. "You think I like climbing up that braid every day? You know how tempting this is?" She pulled out a necklace with a silver key dangling on the loop.

"The key to the elevator!" Fiona said.

Frieda had been sitting quietly, thinking. At last she spoke. "I don't understand. Aren't you a mean witch?"

"As sure as the spider spins, I am!" Violet said. "I was a star student at the Black Magic Witch Academy, but I was always different from the others. You see, being a mean witch is rather lonely. That's why when I had the chance to be the mean witch from *Rapunzel,* I jumped at it."

"Why?" Fiona asked.

"Well, what other witch has the chance to have a daughter?" Violet said. "Plus, I had to protect Rapunzel. I didn't want another really mean witch to get the part."

"But you stole me from my parents!" Rapunzel said.

"Oh, my sweet little fruit bat," Violet said, pulling Rapunzel onto her lap. "That's why I never wanted you to read your fairy tale. It's so full of upsetting errors."

"You mean you didn't kidnap Rapunzel?" Fiona asked Violet.

"Skeletons, no! Your mother and I were great friends," Violet said to Rapunzel. "We had so many things in common—gardening and cooking. We were always sharing seeds and recipes. Plus," Violet said, smiling at the memory, "we both had the same favorite food . . ."

"Rapunzel!" Fiona and Frieda said together.

"I've wanted to tell you about your parents for so many years," Violet said to Rapunzel. "I suppose you're old enough now to understand." Violet sniffled heavily.

"Theirs was the fate of so many other parents," she continued, with a heavy sigh.

"You mean they're dead?" Fiona said.

"Lost at sea collecting sand dollars for Rapunzel's dowry," Violet said, sniffling again. "It was up to me to raise you after that and to continue the fairy tale as best I could."

A hush fell over the room as each person thought her own thoughts.

The girls looked at Violet and Rapunzel curled up together on Rapunzel's hair. They certainly did look more like a mom and a daughter than a damsel and a witch. What kind of fairy tale was this anyway? No dresses! Not a cackle! And, with Rapunzel's terrible singing voice, maybe not even a prince! Was this fairy tale even worth saving?

And yet . . . memories of yesterday started flooding Fiona and Frieda's minds. They'd climbed a braid up the Drop of Doom! They'd had a pajama party with a maiden who could hit a ball out of the stadium—if she'd ever get the chance. They'd bravely faced a mean witch! Okay, a nice witch, but still a witch with magic powers—and a really sweet lady. And weren't they glad for that?

As much as they wanted to help Rapunzel, they couldn't live with her until the prince showed up. They needed Violet to stay with her.

This fairy tale hadn't turned out the way they'd expected at all, but even so—

"Don't do it," Frieda suddenly said. "Don't cut off Rapunzel's hair."

"Don't send her away!" Fiona said. "Stay here and take care of each other."

"But what about the fairy tale?" Violet asked. "I just don't know. We'll be disappointing so many girls . . ."

"But don't you see?" Frieda said. "We like this story *better*."

"You do?" Violet looked amazed.

"Besides," Fiona said. "You can find other ways to make it interesting."

"I like that idea!" Rapunzel said.

She grabbed her doodle-covered notebook. "Let's brainstorm!" she said. F & F & R & V's NEW, INTERESTING ENDINGS, she wrote across the top.

"Number One," she read out loud as she wrote, "R becomes famous shortstop. Hits ball all the way to Arctic Circle. Meets prince, famous walrus-tamer, on ice floe."

"Ah-ha-haaaa-haaaa!" At that, Violet laughed so hard she let out a real-live witchy cackle. "Number Two," she said, "mean witch climbs Mount Everest!"

"You wish!" Frieda said, poking Violet's arm.

"Number Three," Fiona chimed in, "Fiona and Frieda get to ride the Drop of Doom!"

"That's what I was going to say!" Frieda said.

And so, for one last time, Violet climbed down Rapunzel's braid. She pulled out the silver key from around her neck, turned it in the ignition, and—

"Wooo-hoooo-wooooooo-hoooooo-hooooooo!"

It was official. Fiona and Frieda had truly had the time of their lives. Later, when they left the magic realm of fairy tales and met back up with Fiona's mom, they could honestly tell her that they had not run into *any* problems they couldn't handle.

As for Rapunzel and Violet, they liked living on top of the Drop of Doom, once the elevator was turned back on. Rapunzel really did get to be the shortstop for the Sprinkledust Sprites. She never cut her hair, even though the team had to make an extra-large batting helmet for her. She never stopped hitting baseballs out her window, either.

In fact, one rainy day, Rapunzel was doing her batting practice from the tower when a young man heard a mysterious cracking sound. *Is that someone batting a ball?* he wondered. (He was a baseball player himself, so he recognized the sound.)

He followed the noise to Rapunzel's tower and, in amazement, watched the balls fly far, far across the field. He fell in love with Rapunzel at first sight.

Many years later, he and Rapunzel were married on the pitcher's mound of the Sprinkledust Sprites baseball stadium. Fiona, Frieda, and Violet were so happy, they cried like three leaky spray guns. And that's the story of how Rapunzel and the prince—and the not-so-mean witch—lived happily ever after.

The End

#6. Lettuce leaves,
short sleeves!

#10. Chocolate malt,
extra salt!

#14. Ferris wheel,
pig squeal!